George H. Hopkins

The Circuit Rider on Foot

My first year in the ministry

George H. Hopkins

The Circuit Rider on Foot
My first year in the ministry

ISBN/EAN: 9783337387655

Printed in Europe, USA, Canada, Australia, Japan

Cover: Foto ©Andreas Hilbeck / pixelio.de

More available books at **www.hansebooks.com**

The Circuit Rider on Foot,

OR,

My First Year in the Ministry.

BY

Rev. GEORGE H. HOPKINS,

———

ROCKFORD, ILL.:
A. F. JUDD & CO , PRINTERS AND ENGRAVERS
1890.

DEDICATION.

To my Christian mother, whose prayers are ever for my success in my chosen field of labor, is this volume lovingly dedicated

By The Author.

PREFACE.

Dear reader, this is my first effort at book-making. I do not know as one's experience become as interesting to others as to self. What one knows for himself may be of more worth to self than to any one else. Be that as it may, there may be great lessons drawn from other's experience. It certainly can do no harm to tell what one has known for himself in the line of duty. A minister's life is sometimes looked upon as an easy life. Some even think that is a pleasureable life, with little care and plenty to eat and wear. If there is any pleasure in the ministry it is not in the fact one is a minister, but rather in the fact that the duties of the office are performed to the best of one's ability. If there is a state of ease to one in the work it is the ease of conscience and not mortal laziness. A preacher's life is not a life of no cost and all pay. I have long since learned that there is more imaginary pleasure than real pleasure in all human things. If one thinks it is better to be a minister than a farmer, or a mechanic, he will surely find that one place is no easier than another in this world, if one is filling the station assigned to him. Even a man sitting on a dry goods box in front of a store "of a long summer day," is a man whose life is the most burdensome and whose task if done well wearies him more than the hard labor of the farm would. He always seems to be tired, too. There is but a certain amount of earthly comfort for a man in this life. If one seeks pleasure in idleness he finds himself sadly disappointed in his pursuit. If he seeks it in labor, he is happier while toiling, although he thinks that ease would be a greater pleasure. But the truth is that God's richest and brightest blessings are wrapped up in hearty service. So the ministry is not the exception to the rule. Its greatest blessings come from the hardest toil and the severest strain.

The chosen vessel must be broken that the streams may flow. The smitten rock sent forth the pure and sparkling water, and the crucified Redeemer brought life and immortality to light. Had there been no death and burial there could have been no Resurrection dawn. So in all the great work of the ministry the submission to suffering and hardship and trial is the power that opens the gates and floods the world with the glory of saving grace and matchless love.

If a man thinks the minister of the gospel has an easy time of it he does not consider the nature of things or the nature of that service the minister is called to perform.

He does not read well the gospel story, nor does he dis-
cover the many paralellisms that must exist between a
suffering Christ and a sacrificing ministry. The work of
a preacher is not a self-imposed task, but with all of his
misgivings he cries with Paul "Woe is me, if I preach not
the gospel." He enters the work as a servant of the Lord
Jesus Christ, who dare not disobey except he forfeit his
peace of mind and rest of soul.

His service must not depend upon what others say or
do, for while he is ministering to a faulty people, and a
fault-finding people, and even a rebellious people, he must
do the bidding of the Lord whether others like it or not.
He has but one to please and that is God.

In writing this book I have tried to the best of my
ability to recall all of the incidents of interest to others
Some things are not as fully described as they might have
been. It would take too long to tell all, and then the
intention of the author in writing this book is not to
enlarge upon or follow up everything to the last limit, but
simply to give a good and fair synopsis of a minister's
trials and triumphs during one brief year.

However it may appear to others, it is to the author
a year of such important lessons that it cannot fail to
linger in memory as one of the most sacred of treasures.
What does a man value more than childhood's happy
hours that hang upon the walls of memory encased in
gold never to be taken down? Why does he prize those
memories? Because they are the days of the beginnings
of things. The morning dawn of every-day life and
experience. The days wherein petty trials and brimming

joys flitted like birds on wings. We cannot forget the beginnings. So to the minister of the gospel in his first year, it is the infancy of a new life, and it must write itself upon the heart in letters of light, there to stay. It is a reality beyond any and every question, and becomes at once the rock-bed of all future efforts and the alphabet of a science that grows in magnitude as years go by. It is the nucleus around which all subsequent history must cluster, and a book of reference to which one oft refers in times of doubt or fear. Such to the author, at least, has been the experience of that first year in the ministry.

If it can be a help to others on the sea of life, the effort will well pay the author. Let no one think for one moment that the author considers this narrative of facts anything unparalelled in human experience. Thousands of ministers, living to-day, of my age, no doubt have material at hand that would be more marvelous than anything written in this book. Read it, please, simply as the story of a Methodist minister's experience in early life and during a first year in that noble work; not as what a man did simply, or endured, but as the result of a Divine support given to mortal man.

What I was able to do was through the assistance of the Divine Master. I was nothing but a man, not a *superhuman*, but a *human* being. Some expect of human beings in the ministry superhuman work and superhuman perfection, but a minister is not an angel yet, but he hopes to be some day. You will not be able to find any wings under the preacher's coat. Do not expect too much of your preacher. Credit him with humanity and treat him as such in love for the sake of the Master.

So with these few words I must leave you to wade through the rest of the book as best you can, and that you will not find in wading any place too deep for you to keep your chin above water, or at least your eyes, is the wish of the author.

GEO. H. HOPKINS.

MY EARLY LIFE.

I was born in the state of————; so to begin with I am a "Yankee," and the son of a "Yankee," and the grand son of a "Yankee,"—an old-fashioned "down-Easter;" for my great grand father lived in the state of Rhode Island and there my grandfather was born. He grew up in that state and in Connecticut, and lived there in the days of the "old blue laws."

My mother was also an American, but how far back in her ancestry the American blood dated I can not say. She was brought up as a Baptist of the "hard-shell" kind, and, not liking that order of ecclesiastics, she united with the Methodist Episcopal church, when she was converted. She was always an ardent advocate of the Methodist doctrines and a firm believer in God and the Bible. Her all was laid upon the altar, even her family. She always kept her little ones in the Sabbath school. She began with them very early in life to teach them, and educate them in the Christian faith. Her children were not left to grow up and then choose for themselves whether they would go to Sabbath school or not, nor to be invited to attend by some Sunday-school missionary; but she had her children in the Sunday school before they were big enough to even dress their feet. I cannot remember when I first went to Sabbath school and to church. It would be impossible for me to swear positively that I had not always been there. If a person should come up and swear that I was born in a church, I should be about ready to concede to it, for my earliest recollections are, that I was there. So, for all practical purposes, I have always been to Sunday-school, and always belonged to the church, and my first breath must have been a prayer my mother taught me.

I would not have any one think that I am an angel or a remarkable saint, for I fear I am not even good enough to be worthy to stand among the angels and saints in the next world. I am only a weak, sinning mortal, and unless God can overlook my great mistakes and follies I would stand a very poor chance of a crown and a robe and a home. My mother did her duty with her children, but that did not remove my sinful tendencies, nor make me a clean boy. I was a little sinner, wicked and rebellious, and quarreling with my brothers and sisters and play-mates, and always into mischief; and, as my people often told me, I never could hold still for one minute of time. I never caught but one contagious disease, and that one "the measles." The only reason they could give for my escaping, while all the rest of the family were sick with everything that came along, was simply that *I "could*

never hold still long enough to catch any disease.'' So, if
that is the true cause of my escapes, I think I am more to
be praised than to be blamed for "keeping on the move."
But I was a thoughtless, pleasure-loving and pleasure-
seeking boy, and at the age of twelve years I attended a
revival meeting in my native town, and there I gave my
heart to God. They invited sinners to come to the altar,
and, on the evening in question, I thought that invitation
was for me, and while they were singing that sweet hymn
of invitation: "Come Ye Sinners Poor and Needy," and
the chorus, "Turn to the Lord and Seek Salvation, Sound
the Praise of His Dear Name," etc., I arose with others
and went to the altar, and there I found peace and pardon,
and I was very happy in the new experience. I went home
that evening a new boy. The next day I lived a new life,
and my mother and my brothers and sisters could note
the change, as well as I could experience it in my own
heart.

A few years after this change, either three or four, I
attended a camp-meeting, and there God called me to the
work of the ministry. I gave myself up to God there and
then to be anything that the Lord willed, and then it was
that God sent down his Holy Spirit and filled the cup to
over-flowing. I was the happiest being on the old camp
ground. And years after, as I passed the old camp ground,
I thought of that wonderful blessing, and turned aside to
find the spot where I erected my Ebenezer. I found the
old tree, and the very spot where heaven and earth seemed
to meet, and where angels mingled with saints.

I left the camp ground at the close of that meeting

with a heart full of love for God and all mankind. The Lord had given me the victory over the flesh and the Devil, and over Hell as well. I went back to my work on the farm with everything about me praising God, and I, myself, doing my "level best" to keep up with creation in thanksgiving to God. It was the "Joy of the Lord," and it was my "strength." I had to drive a large herd of cattle over a high hill every morning to the back of the farm and then go after them again every night, and this afforded me the opportunity to commune with God. One old hickory tree was one of my secret places of prayer, and oft I held the sweetest communion with my God of all my life under the old hickory tree. All of this time I was saying to God, "I will go and preach." I used to look with a great amount of satisfaction upon the calling of God to this high place of service.

The Lord blessed me, and led me, and I was not tempted for a long time. All this time I said: "I will." By and by the Devil tempted me, and I began to consider. That is the point of danger with everyone. When we begin to consider the Devil's proposition, it does not take long for the Devil to get us. I used to fish a great deal when a boy, and some times, when the water was clear, I could see the fish. I noticed sometimes that nice large fish would go swimming by, and I would drop my hook in front of them, and they would dodge off and shoot out into deeper water. If a fish would not stop and examine the bait, or give any attention to it, I knew I could not catch that fish. But, when one would hang around the bait, and run up to it, I was quite certain to catch that fish. So the Devil is quite certain of his fish when the fish stops to look at the bait.

The Devil finally made me think that anything else was better than the ministry. I said: "I will not," and, when I said that, I was going away from God. And then the pendulum swung from "*I will*" to "*I will not*" and back again, and so on. And for two or three years, I was religious and then irreligious, pious and impious, hot, and then cold. Sometimes a Methodist preacher would be an honorable title, and then the last thing to ever think of being. It was good, bad and indifferent. I would be a school-teacher, a lawyer, a politician—anything except a Methodist preacher. And thus the struggle went on, while I was trying to chose a calling for life. A moment-ous question that. Many a man has turned the switch and gone the wrong road at that point. It is a great thing for a young man to find his place,—the one that he is best adapted to fill, and then to make the most of him-self in his place. I realize now the danger and perils at-tendant upon the wrong choice of a profession. Not that I made any mistake in my choice, but from what I am, and what I might have been, I am able to see how many snares were set for my feet. But thank God for one thing: there are no snares for the feet of those who walk the road to duty.

While this struggle was going on, I had even made a choice against my convictions of duty, but in keeping with my every desire, as I then felt. I made up my mind that I would be a lawyer. I thought that I would be ashamed to be called a Methodist preacher, but not to be called a lawyer. So into a law office I went, and began the study of the law. I began with Blackstone's Commentary. I read and re-read, and I got more knowledge of duty between the lines, than I did of common law on the lines.

Every day, that I entered the law office, I was remind- of my duty to God, as I crossed the threshold. In order to keep down these convictions, I would not attend the prayer-meetings, nor the class-meetings. An "*I-will-not*" never gets any good going to prayer-meetings anyway. The "*I-will-nots*" never have any prayer-meetings nor anything else very religious. I was simply a poor kind of a Sunday Christian. I went to church on Sunday, when it was easier to go than stay away.

Not because I did not fear God, did I get so icy about religious things; but, because it was hard to force a rebellion against conviction, when on God's territory. That is why the saint meets with saints, and the sinner meets with sinners. That is just why the dutiful child can look up into God's face and smile at the eternal judge, while the guilty sinner cries for the "Rocks and mountains to hide" him from the face of the mighty God of heaven and earth. Duty looks up into God's face, while unfaith- fulness hangs its head in shame and expects to get condemnation from the start. An unfaithful man in religion is not half a man anywhere you may put him. He is a dwarf and a pigmy beside other men. He can be ever so great otherwise, but if untrue to conviction, he must ever have the consciousness with him that being un- true to himself he is even so to all who estimate him as true. Self-respect, then, must be at the very foundation of every sincere person, for no person can respect himself for being a hypocrite.

After a number of months of study of Common Law, mixed with Divine Law and deep conviction, I was nearer a Methodist preacher than when I began the law, and I knew more about my feelings and my duty at the close of my law study, than I did about Blackstone.

Sometime in the summer of that year I thought over my course, and of my neglect of prayer meetings, and I made up my mind that I would go for once to the meeting. I went and tried to do my duty, but, of course, it was formal, as long as I said "*I will not.*" After the meeting, however, the preacher came to me and said: "You will never be a lawyer, God has a work for you to do." "Well," I said, "I do not think that I shall leave the law office until I have finished my course." It did not do me any good to try to cover up my own convictions, when God would tell some one else about them. I did not know how to account for this preacher coming to me and saying what he did, except that God was on my track, and was bound to have me. I went to my room that night deeply moved. I went to the prayer-meeting, and my conscience was condemning me more than ever. I went to the office the next morning, but it was harder than ever before to get my thoughts upon the contents of the book. At last, I threw down the book and started out to call upon the preacher, and tell him my convictions, and turn on the Lord's side. I was almost at the parsonage, when the Devil came and pictured out to me all of the great things in store for me in the world, and reminded me of the prospect of making money; and how I was already beginning to earn money in the office; and that a Methodist preacher was always poor, and was made fun of by the world. Then I turned around and went back to the office, and went to work again. Not many days after, however, I gave up; and when I said, "*I will*" the light shown in again, and I was happy in God. The world was a new world. The birds sang sweeter, the flowers looked more beautiful, and the sun shone brighter and more golden than ever before. And yet the change was not in nature, but in my heart. I was in harmony with everything, when in accord with my God. People, who can not find anything beautiful in this world, have nothing beautiful in themselves. To a saint this world is good enough for present living, and, to a sinner the same world is a dull and meaningless thing; and, because unappreciated, it is too good for him.

After the struggle was over, the thought of going out to preach the gospel demanded some attention. The Discipline and the Bible were my constant study. Every day, and, in fact, every time I took up the Bible, I had to turn to the twenty-third Psalm, and read it. I had never read anything so sweet and comforting as that. It was the very language of my heart. The Discipline is only the condensed milk of the word. And, next to the Bible, the preacher wants the Discipline.

MY FIRST APPOINTMENT.

CHAPTER II.

In the fall I attended conference for the first time, being recommended to the conference for admission on trial. It was a different kind of association from what I was used to. Instead of lawyers, criminals and hangers-on of the law, I was in the company of a large body of clean-hearted, pure-minded and pure-mouthed men. I had been in the habit of smoking cigars, and mingling with smokers. Here in this company there was no tobacco smoke, and nothing unbecoming. I do not mean to be understood to say that lawyers are bad men; for there are plenty of good men in that body of professionals, and pure.minded men too; but a person in law business comes in contact with a great many more bad men, than the majority of the people outside of the profession are aware of. Neither do I mean to infer about preachers, that they do not smoke. For, (I am sorry to say it,) there are many who use tobacco, and very freely too, that go out to preach; and, yet, as a class of men, I can truthfully say, there are more clean men than in any other body of professionals that ever assemble. I do not mean to cast any reflection upon those who use tobacco, neither would I condemn them; but I can say for myself that when I went into the ministry I felt that I must give up my tobacco, and I did so with the help of the Lord.

The session of conference lasted a week; and, at the close of that session, when the appointments were read, I was appointed to the W—— circuit, in the A——District, W——— conference. I was in some doubt about getting work that fall, thinking that perhaps others could be found better fitted for the work than I was. So, when my name was read out by the Bishop, the Spirit of the Lord came upon me, and I knew that God would go with me to my first field of labor. After learning where my circuit was located and how to get there, I started for that place. I felt from the moment the Spirit came upon me that I was going to have a revival on my charge; and so I told the brethren, to their astonishment, before I left the conference. I was as certain of the fact of a revival as though I had been through the struggle. It was no wonder that the preachers looked a little surprised at the prediction. I was prophesying about a work on a field that I was unacquainted with, and did not know there was such a place until I heard it read out by the Bishop in association with my name; and, as a consequence, did not know where it was. But that others doubted my statement did not change my mind about the revival which I was going to have on my circuit.

Well, I reached my circuit in due time, and went to the house of a local preacher to stay my first night. The local preacher, of course, soon learned of my line of work. I told him I was going to have a revival, but he thought I was sort of an enthusiast. His old father lived with him, and he began to laugh at me for saying I was going to have a revival. I had never been on a charge before, and I knew nothing about church work or revival meetings. All that I did know about the work was from studying the Bible and Discipline. So the old man had some little show of argument against me. Finally he said: "You are only a little boy preacher, and what do you know about work? Old gray-haired men have tried to have revivals here and failed, and now you, a boy preacher, come on here without knowing anything about the place or the work, and talk about holding a revival meeting." Well, I said, God is greater than the gray hairs, and I am going to have a revival. I *knew* I was.

The local preacher and his father and the whole family, in fact, were somewhat incensed against me, because I would persist in talking revival.

The next day was Saturday, and I was expected to go out to the farthest limit of my circuit to preach my first sermon on a circuit, and the third one of all. It may be well to give a description of the circuit right here. It consisted of seven appointments. The place where the local preacher lived was headquarters for the whole charge. As I am anxious to furnish no clue to the field of labor, for many reasons, I shall use fictitious names for the different appointments. The first place to be described is head-quarters, and we will call it Yale. This place was composed of a hotel, that had a lively trade over the bar; a store and postoffice, combined, a blacksmith shop, a saw-mill, a school-house, a church, (M. E. church) and a few dwellings, perhaps a dozen. It was on the main road to a thriving town where a number of large tanneries were doing a vast business, and the most of the hemlock bark for these large tanneries went through Yale. The most of the bark-haulers were Catholic Irish, and although there are plenty of good, industrious, sober people in that church, yet, the whole raft of these haulers were hard drinkers. Yale was just far enough from the tanneries to permit the men to get very dry again by the time they could reach there from town. So fighting, swearing, drinking and running horses were everyday occurrences there. And the hotel-keeper was getting rich; as many a poor man left the price of his load of bark with the bar-keeper, as he loaded him on to his wagon and started him home dead-drunk. The next place was Jones, a place about five miles east of Yale. It was a school-house ap-pointment where about fifteen or twenty would turn out to meeeting on a fair day. Another point was Tallman about two miles south of Yale, a school-house appoint-ment. At this place I always had a full house. Then four miles east of this place I had another appointment,—The Maple school-house. And then seven miles south of Yale I had another little village appointment which we will call Graves. Here, also, they had a hotel, two stores, a grist mill and sawmill, a blacksmith shop, a school-house and about a dozen dwelling houses. The people were good-hearted people, but took no interest in religion. Three miles farther south from Graves was the Baker ap-pointment. Here we had a little class of half a dozen members. It was situated in a little ravine where three or four streams came together and formed the S——river, one of the principal rivers of the state of B——. The next and last one of the appointments was Arnold. Here were half a dozen houses, a school-house a hotel, con-verted into a shoeshop, and a dwelling, and one store,— all shut in by the hills. This place was fourteecn miles

THE BAKER SCHOOL-HOUSE.

from headquarters. So the circuit was some five miles wide and fourteen miles long. As I have already stated, I was to preach my first sermon at the Arnold appointment, fourteen miles out. Saturday came and with it the rain in abundance. I had no horse, and as the local preacher did not offer a horse nor to accompany me himself, and take me there, I had to go afoot and alone. I suppose the local preacher did not like something said by me, but I do not know to this day, (unless it was my talking revival,) what it was.

Anyway, with three or four horses in the barn, he allowed me to start off on foot with a thin overcoat and leaky boots without any rubbers, a heavy rain pouring down and very muddy roads. I walked seven miles to Graves, and, when I got there, I was well-soaked. I went into the store at this place and the merchant, finding out who I was, invited me to stay to dinner and "dry off a little," and he would try and get a ride for me. The teams all went the other way that day; so after dinner I started out again on my journey. The roads were flooded in some places, and I had to walk on logs and rails sometimes. When I reached the next place, which was Baker, I felt as though I ought to "hang up to dry." But the next day was my first Sabbath in the work, and so I steamed ahead for the next place. When I came within two miles of Arnold, I stopped at the house of a good Methodist to stay over night, if possible, but the old folks were away and the girls were at home alone. They invited me in and built up a big fire in the old elevated-oven stove and tried to dry the young preacher. But the hotter it got the more

I steamed; and after eating a lunch I started for the "burg." The rain instead of "*letting up*" was "*letting down;*" and, when I reached the old hotel stand, I was taken in by the good lady of the house, who was a whole-souled Methodist, and I rested after a day of queer and wet experiences. I was more of a Baptist than a Methodist that day; or, if a Methodist, I had endured an overdose of sprinkling. The good sister finding the young preacher wet and cold, fired up the kitchen stove "seven times hotter than it was wont to be heated" and brought the old man's best suit out, shirt and all, for me to put on. After I had changed my clothes, she collected the wet clothes and hung them around the hot stove, until it looked as though the young preacher had been cut up to dry. The boots had no shine and no shape, and it took the united efforts of two to get the preacher out of his boots. This was my introduction as a circuit rider, and, moreover, I was a *circuit rider on foot.* I fulfilled part of the scripture anyway, for I came by water. That was a peculiar introduction to the ministry. There was combined in it Methodist *zeal*, Baptist *soaking*, Presbyterian *go-through-to-the-end*, Episcopalian *go-it-alone* and Universalistic *come-out-all-right-in-the-end*. Getting into some stained, streaked, crimped and shrunken clothes and more shrunken boots the next morning, I was ready to preach my first sermon on a circuit.

MY FIRST SABBATH ON A CHARGE.

CHAPTER III.

It had ceased to rain when the morning dawned, and, although the roads were very muddy, there was a goodly number out to the morning service at the school-house at Arnold. We had a good time at that first meeting, and the Lord blessed us all. That meeting alone paid me for my trouble the day before. The Lord paid me double wages for walking in the mud and rain fourteen miles. Then I started back, after eating a hasty dinner, on the road I traveled the day before. The afternoon appointment was at Baker. I waded mud and water, and leaped mudholes and little streams, and walked logs and rails, and all the time praising God and singing old Methodist hymns. The Baker appointment was a school-house appointment. But it was not more than *half* a school-house. The little, old school-house had one row of seats on each side extending from the aisle to the wall. The seats had been whittled and carved and bored through with jack-knives until they hardly held together. There were, I think, a dozen of such seats, all told, in the room. Then the teacher's desk and platform must have been built in the days when it was safe for the pedagogue to have something to hide behind at certain times. I used to call it "the box stall." There were two steps to get up to the platform, which was very narrow, so that, between the side of the building and the rough board desk, (built of boards set on end with a board flat on top for a table) there was hardly room to be seated comfortably without turning sidewise; and, even then the seat was a narrow board fastened to the side of the house. Once seated behind this, one could just see over the top of it and take good aim at the heads of those in the back seats. It was a sort of "*rifle pit*" in times of rebellion. Then again, the school-house had been built way down in the lot, at least a quarter of a mile from the road, so that travelers could go by without having to run much risk, probably. When I arrived at this little, old house, I found eight or ten in the room waiting to hear the new preacher, and "*size him up.*" I climbed up into the teacher's place and took a seat, to shield me from the sharp eyes of my congregation, and I found the desk not only serviceable in that respect, but, also it served to hide my feet, so that they could not see how big my feet were, nor how muddy my boots were, nor how many wrinkles I had in my pants, nor how I had them plastered over with mud. So, with such good protection, I was in shape to preach my second sermon. I did the best I could with wet feet. After the meeting was over I went to the house of a good Methodist brother and had some supper and dried my feet, so that I could get them wet again going to the next place.

The evening appointment was at Graves. When I reached there, I found a good number out. The largest audience of the day. It was a school-house, and, when I came within a number of rods of the house, I could hear the roar within. It sounded some like the mighty waves of the ocean dashing against the rocks, and, sometimes, like the rumbling of a great mill. I was almost afraid to open the door, for fear the Lion would jump out at me. I stood outside for a few minutes scraping and rubbing to get the mud off and get all of the kinks out of my pants and coat, which seemed to bear marks of the washing I gave them the day before. That was quite a suspense to me as I stood outside. I got hold of the door and slowly pushed it open and glided up onto the platform, which was between the two doors. I had before me a rough and noisy crowd of good hearted people. They looked me over from head to foot and from left to right, and tried to see my back; but nature has one good law that prevents a man turning a corner with his vision. He can not see behind the pulpit nor see the many wrinkles in the back of the preacher's coat, when the preacher is facing the audi-ence. I do not know what I said that night in particular, but the general run of my talk was what I considered the duty of a Methodist preacher. I feared that they came to the conclusion that night that the performance of my duty in Graves would not be conducive to the highest pleasure of the pleasure-loving people of that place, for that was the only time I saw that audience in that school-house for six months, or more. But I learned in time that they always went to hear the first and last sermon a preacher delivered there, and were thus able to tell how much a man could or did improve in a year. That night I went and staid with a merchant,—a good, liberal and friendly man. His home was always open to a Method-ist preacher. All of the people were very friendly and made the preacher welcome, but they had no time to go to church. That night I slept with the consciousness of having done all I could for the Master. But it was a poor service. I believe the Lord blessed me more for my four-teen miles walk in the rain and mud the day before, than for the sermons I tried to preach on Sunday; for I was used to walking and knew how to do it, but I was not used to preaching God's word, and knew not how to preach it. I know I was accepted of God, however, for I had done all I was able to do, and that is acceptable to God at anytime.

MY FIRST REVIVAL.

CHAPTER IV.

The headquarters of the circuit were at Yale appointment, where was built the only church on the circuit. At this place the local preacher lived. I began my work as the Discipline requires, visiting from house to house and praying with the people. I was very timid when I began my work, and sometimes I have stood on the doorstep of a house and could hardly muster up courage enough to knock on the door or ring a bell; and after knocking, I have felt my heart come up in my throat and my knees shake like wicked Belshazzar's when he saw the handwriting on the wall. Once in a house and seated, I hardly knew what to do with myself. It was very hard, also, to ask the privilege of having prayer with a family before going away. I have staid many times, during my first year, an hour longer than I wanted to just trying to get brave enough to ask the privilege of prayer.

Late in the fall I announced at the church revival
meetings. The rain came down in torrents on the first
night of the meetings, and the brethren present, including
the local preacher and his father, thought it better not to
hold meetings at present. They thought I ought to wait
until the roads were better and the rain over. To tell the
truth about the matter, the local preacher and his father
and a few others were not in favor of my holding meetings anyway. I finally consented to postpone the meetings for one week, but this did not please them altogether.
I was certain of victory and so I would obey God rather
than man. So the next week I appointed meetings again,
and the rain came also; in fact it had been coming all of
the time for two or three weeks. The local preacher and
his father were on hand, but growled, and perhaps they
came that night to get in their growl. Rain or no rain,
roads or no roads, I had started a through train that
time, and I did not need any brakeman on that train.
The meetings increased day after day, and the mud too.
I secured a good brother to help me in the meetings, and
when the work was over we counted seventy conversions.
The people came for miles around. They came with horse
teams and ox teams, on horseback and on foot, some in
lumber wagons, some on "buckboards" and some in ox
carts. And probably some did not come anyway.

Well, after such a work as that sometimes there comes
in a devil to "help string the fish," as they say. There
were more people outside of the Methodist church
professing to enjoy religion, that were continually making
preparations to "string the fish" than were actually en-

THE YALE CHURCH.

gaged in trying to catch the fish. The Free Methodist church had a fish string and were anxious to string some of the fish. The Protestant Methodist church was extremely anxious in regard to the stringing of the fish. Then the First and Second Day Adventists and the Seventh Day Baptists, although they did not "*go a-fishing*" with us, rather laid claim to some of the spoils, and so they came in to do their best to "string the most fish." It did look at one time as though they had came to a mutual agreement among themselves that he should be branded the "*best fellow*" who could get the most proselytes, and that the Seventh Day Baptist preachers, (for they had sometimes three of their preachers on hand,) and the Free Methodist preacher and the Protestant preacher were in the ring for the prize. I sometimes thought they would overthrow the whole work. I trusted in God to help me through and care for my interest. I never did any proselyting, and when the others had gone far enough with it I "opened fire" on their old fortifications and made them mad. When the smoke of battle cleared away I had the privilege of taking into the Methodist church the best part of the converts; and they came of their own free will too.

One of the young men converted in the meetings leaned toward our church and would have joined, but the Seventh Day Baptists persuaded him that the true Sabbath was Saturday, and so he finally "turned his coat" and went to keeping Saturday for Sunday. I am afraid they read their Bibles backwards and bottom-side up too. The spirit of that ecclesiastical body is quite truthfully portrayed in the story of Don Quixote, who knew nothing outside of certain books. So the Saturday worshipers lay more stress upon the day than the Gospel of Christ; and it is because they read the Old Testament with the "vail upon their hearts." Some people like to be out of joint with the rest of the world, and they are always an insignificant minority. It is like the man questioning the drowning boy about his falling in the water, and chiding him for getting into deep water, rather than trying to help him out and save his life. All a drowning man wants is rescue. These false teachers that strain at a gnat and swallow a camel will wake up some day. While souls are dying all around us a man has no business with anything that will not help a soul out of danger and to Christ.

In order to train this young man in their faith, and, also, to keep him in the right way, one of the members of that church employed him to work for him. But I fear the Devil got him at last. He had been regarded as a steady, honest young man. A strange thing, however, happened in connection with this young proselyte. The man he worked for, who was the main man in the Seventh Day Baptist class, had a number of things stolen one night, including a large ham. No one seemed to know anything about them, and there was no clue to the stolen property. Not long after this a fire was discovered in a pile of lumber, in the center of a lot belonging to this young man, and parties going to put out the fire discovered the stolen property in the lumber pile, ham and all. This young man had stolen them without any earthly use for them, not even for the ham, unless to make a meat-offering of it to the gods of the Seventh Day, which he was trying to do, using his lumber pile as an altar and fuel. Ashamed of what he had done, and failing to burn out the evidence of his guilt, either in the community or the church or his conscience, he left the country, while an old father and mother were left behind filled with shame and sorrow. That was the end of a Seventh Day Baptist proselyte.

The Free Methodists succeeded in getting two members of the M. E. church to go off with them. The church they left was no worse off without them nor weaker, either financially or spiritually, and if the other church gained anything by the accessions, I hardly think anybody envied them their gain. So amid all the struggle and through it all the M. E. church lost no strength with God's help. The work over here, I was now ready for meetings at another point, and thither I went full of faith and the Holy Ghost.

REVIVAL AT THE TALLMAN SCHOOL HOUSE.

CHAPTER V.

The people of Tallman neighborhood were good-hearted people but rather rude, some of them, and very much in need of a revival. When I contemplated going to Tallman to start meetings, the local preacher was as much opposed to my going there as he was to my starting meetings at Yale. He thought the people were too wicked for me to do anything *with* or *for* them, but such shallow counsel on such shallow reasons was altogether to thin for me to waste five minutes to even hear him talk. So I treated his advice just as people do slops on a wash day, I threw it away. The meetings commenced, continued and ended in a rain storm. We had rain in place of snow about all winter. The work started with a good interest and we were having good work done; souls were being converted, and among the rest a poor drunkard for whom a faithful wife had long prayed. She came three miles afoot in rain and mud to get to the meetings and God saved her husband and some of her children. When the meetings were at this high pitch of interest the Devil undertook to overthrow it. The local preacher had a hand in it, I am sorry to say, for through a friend of his he sought to close the school-house against us. If I had an enemy the same was always a friend of the local P. They agitated the matter thoroughly throughout the neighborhood, and then came to the meeting. and the friend of the local preacher was "spokesman." He arose about the close of the meeting and said that it w as the sentiment of the district that the meetings should not continue longer in the house.

"Well," I said, "the majority of the people who are interested are here, and I guess I will put it to a vote."

So I called for a vote of the people on the question, and only four or five voted against the meetings continuing. That ended the matter as to the use of the house, so the enemy had to sharpen his tools and attack us at another point.

The meetings were thrown open for all to take part who desired, so the enemy thought he would try us at that point. The next thing was to find a man for a tool. There was living about three miles from the schoolhouse a very rough old man who hated preachers, Methodist preachers especially, and a lover of the Devil and a practitioner of his Satanic arts. He had some learning and a boasted ability to outwit any preacher in the country. He was one of those preacher-tormenters, and a hard case. It was like Goliah of Gath going out to meet little David. He was a big, surly fellow, with a fist big enough for a mawl, almost, and a foot to match. They invited him to come down to the meeting and talk, as I allowed the privilege for all to speak that so desired. So the "*old tar*" came down bent on mischief. I held my meeting as usual, and preached a sermon that pricked the old man a little without knowing that I had done it. When the meeting was thrown open to all, the old man took his place on the floor and began contradicting my sermon. After he finished I arose and put the answer in the form of an appeal to the audience as to which side of the case they would be willing to run the risk of an eternity. The result was better gained thus than by any contradiction. The old man could not stand that kind of repulse in silence, so he arose to speak again, and his voice seemed to change until it sounded like the roar of a mad bull or a caged lion. He was frightened and so were his friends, for they knew not what to make of the change. I arose and called him to order, and said to him: "Mr.——, if what you are going to say, you are certain will help any one to live a better life or reform, you can speak on, otherwise, I want you to take your seat and keep still." It is evident that he did not think his talk would do anyone any good, for he took his seat, but in a rage. He came two or three nights to the meeting, and every time he came he was a worse man than before. Finally he raved so much that he frightened many of the women. His friends were backing him up still, for they hated to suffer a defeat. So they arranged for a meeting and had the old man announce it in my meeting, appointing it the next night, on my own night, too. So I took up my

appointment for that night, for I could do no other way
without sore trouble. The old man was to preach. Some
of the Christian people wanted to know what I was going
to do, and I told them I was going to the meeting. So
we went, a goodly number of the Christian people. The
"*old tar*" came in and threw down his hat with a good
deal of force upon the desk and said something that
made some of them laugh. He then pulled off his big
overcoat and threw it on the floor, and took a chair and
looked over the crowd. The Devil had begun his revival.
I took a seat in the audience to see the end, if there should
be any end that night. The old fellow arose and began
by saying something about the young preacher. Then
he began one of the most abusive harangues that one
would care to listen to. He abused me as much as he
could, and even threatened my life. Then he tried to show
that I did not preach the Bible, as I claimed to do. So he
selected a chapter and tried to read it, but he could not
read the first line of the first verse; so, one of his backers,
a little Englishman, who thought himself smarter than
most of the people, went up to read the chapter for the
old man, but it seemed as though God choked him down,
for he could not read the first verse, and had to take his
seat looking very red in the face. I arose and went up
and said to him, "I will read it for you, if you wish."
The fellow took his chair saying, "Yes! Yes!"

Taking the Bible, I said, "Now, my friends, this is
God's word, let us have quiet. I do not ask you to be
quiet simply on my account, but this is God's word, and
I want you to hear what God has to say." They quieted

down and were very still all through the reading of the chapter. After I had taken my seat the old man began to talk again about me, and attempted to prove from the chapter read, that I was all wrong and leading the people astray. I certainly was leading them astray, if he was to be the judge; for we were going another road from what he was. He talked for perhaps a half hour or more, and then took the Bible again to read out of it. He tried to quiet the house, as I had done when I read, but the people only laughed at him. He tried to read, and could not read the selection; so I went up again and read the second chapter for him, which seemed to rather madden than please him, that I could read it and he could not. So about all that he had to say that night was abuse for me and wicked threats of what he would do to me, if I did not stop my preaching there. There ended the Devil's work for that night.

The next night I held my meeting as usual, and after the sermon a very wicked man, a "State's prison bird," as they call an ex-convict, and his wife came forward and were both soundly converted. He said he came the night before to help on the other meeting, and he became convinced that our side was right, and he could see a big difference in the spirit manifested on our side, from that on the other. So the Devil lost some ground in that campaign. We had better work after the battle waxed hot.

A few nights after this I came to the meeting, and found most of the people standing outside of the schoolhouse. On inquiry I learned that the old man was inside, and was seated on the platform, and gave them to know

THE TALLMAN SCHOOL-HOUSE.

that I was not going to have a meeting that night, but
that he was going to have one himself. I walked around
the schoolhouse and found some of his disciples, and
backers, amusing themselves over the prospect. I said to
them, "If you do not take that old man out of that
house, and keep him out, I will have him arrested to-mor-
row." So they went in and led the fellow out and off. We
had no more trouble with him at the school-house. I had
not escaped individually, however, the troublesome old
man of sin, for he would follow me up when visiting, and
abuse me the worst kind. Sometimes he would come
where I stayed over night, before we had finished breakfast, and would yell so that the neighbors could hear him,
and since the first night that he talked at the school-house
his voice was like a lion's roar. The Devil had him, and
the Devil had an abiding place in his heart, too. He finally
became so bad that his friends had to nail him up in his
room to keep him home. His backers were whipped-out,
for they were ashamed of their leader, and ashamed of
their course and of themselves, for causing such trouble
in this old man's family, and in the neighborhood. Our
meetings continued until we were ready to stop them,
and we had many converted. God made the wrath of
man to praise him.

During these meetings we enjoyed much of God's
presence and power. Some of the meetings were wonderful in power. We held the cottage prayer-meetings every
day. Some days it was a spiritual feast all day, and all
night. They had a good custom of reading around at
family altar and all uniting in prayer. So a family altar

was sometimes a real prayer-meeting. One morning I engaged with the family, where I stayed over night, in the family devotions, and then crossing the road I found the neighbor about to have family prayer. They furnished me with a Bible and I joined with them in reading the morning lesson, each one reading a verse from oldest to youngest. Then we all went to praying one after another until all had prayed. A little ways up the road were living a young couple lately converted, and I said to some of them after prayer, "let us go up and help our young couple in their family altar." So off we started. They were just finishing breakfast when we arrived. So we had a glorious time with them as we approached the "mercy seat." That was a morning meal. Then after dinner we had meeting at a house out in a lot, away from any road. Some were sick and unable to go to meeting, so we went over to pray with them, and God sent down the Holy Ghost upon us. There were many shining faces that afternoon. That evening we met at the school-house for our regular revival meeting. We were in good shape for such a work after our day of communion. That night we had a shower of blessings. It seemed that day as if it had been showers upon showers, and blessings as thick as rain drops in a shower, and they fell upon everybody who loved the Lord. Just at the close of the evening meeting, some one proposed another meeting that night two miles away, and some four miles out of the way for some of the earnest ones. Accordingly it was given out, and we started after ten o'clock at night for a cottage prayer-meeting. One poor sister and husband and children came "afoot" to the meetings, and anxious to enjoy the late meeting, decided to walk two miles farther away from home, for the sake of attending this night meeting. The meeting was well-attended, and while we prayed the Lord sent down the Holy Ghost upon us. Everybody in the house was filled with the laughing spirit that night, and they laughed heartily. That meeting was always alluded to as the "laughing meeting." We had the best of the wine at the last of the feast.

Then we had another kind of meeting which I termed "double meetings." I claimed that agreement would bring the Holy Ghost according to the promise; so sometimes we failed to agree. Then, if we had a dull meeting, I would at the close of the meeting begin over as if we had just met for meeting. At one of these meetings, of which I speak, we had prayed, and we had sung, and we had talked, and there was no life in the whole service. An old man and his son were there in the house, both of them ungodly men. I arose as if to close the meeting, and I said to the Christian people, "we came here to get a blessing and to be filled with the Holy Ghost, without which we can do nothing; now, why did not God fulfill his promise? Just because we were not all agreed 'touching one thing.' Now, we will begin all over again, and let as all pray for the descent of the Holy Ghost." We began in earnest to seek for God's blessing and it speedily came, thanks be to God; and some shouted for joy, some laughed, some cried and some were gliding over a sea of glorious calm, and some were praying and praising God. All at once there was a new interest awakened, for the old father and his son were both on their knees pleading for mercy with all their might, without any invitation from us. They gathered around and soon there were two more happy ones that joined our band. That was a happy company indeed.

The lady of the house, although a Christian, had never believed in shouting. The old man that was converted was her father and the young man her brother, so she was extremely happy this night. She stood up and said, "Dear christian friends, I never did believe in shouting, for I thought it was all put on, as they say but I do believe in shouting now, for I feel like it myself; Glory to God!" And she clapped her hands and shouted at the top of her voice. In fact, we all felt like shouting, and done so, too.

At another cottage meeting five young ladies attended the meeting for the first time. We had another double meeting. When I began the second meeting I felt I must speak to those young people. So I arose and went to them, and soon as I would speak to one the tears would come, and when I had spoken to the last one we all knelt down with the rest of the company, for they had not knelt during prayer. But, when they bowed before the Lord, it seemed as though the very windows of heaven were opened and showers fell upon us. The good brother that was praying, when these five ladies knelt down, came across the room on his knees while praying. The place was shaken with the power of God. We had many such meetings.

During some of these meetings some very timid Christians got so that they could pray and speak and shout as the boldest of them, and all became so intensely interested that a meeting five miles away would be attended by those Christian people, even if they had to walk. Among them one sister, (whose husband had been lately converted,) and her family, have been known to go five miles, and walk every step of the way to get to an evening meeting with God's people.

MY EFFORTS TO EVANGELIZE GRAVES.

CHAPTER VI.

The Graves appointment was one of the poorest on the circuit. As stated previously, the people did not go to church. I went to Graves once in two weeks, enduring all sort of fatigue to get there. Sometimes the roads were so bad I was completely tired out by the time I reached Graves. I used to go across lots and over the hills and through the woods about seven miles, and to find no one out to church. I used to open the school-house, and find-the key, which sometimes necessitated my chasing over the town to even get track of it, build the fire and ring the bell, and then stand at the window and watch for someone to come. More times I used to watch in vain than with any degree of satisfaction, during the first six months of the year. After the revival fire had spread pretty much all over the circuit, and I had finished up at other points, I thought I would try and hold a meeting in

Graves. I planned for a big effort, but I had no one else that had faith enough to even attend the meetings. I could not get any of the members of the church to consent to go to Graves to help me. They had no faith and no desire. Everybody, for miles around, seemed to think that Graves was a modern Sodom, and I do not know but some even expected to hear that fire and brimstone had destroyed the place. Some complained because I went there. I concluded to go in the name of the Lord, and do what I could for that people.

I announced meetings in Graves and started in the very next night. Very few came, and I had to sing and pray and speak for the entertainment of the few present. I could not get them out for evening meetings, so I tried a day meeting, in the morning, and then an afternoon meeting, and all to no purpose. One afternoon three ladies came out to see and to hear. So I held a regular service and preached to them the best I could. That was the only day service that I had with anyone else than myself present. All the meetings were "close communion," as I had it all to myself. I would go and open the house, and ring the bell, and when it was time for the meeting, I would sing and pray and go my way until the next appointment. I went from house-to-house to invite them out to meeting, and they all had some excuse. I tried to talk to them, and they would only laugh at me. It was impossible to draw them out in conversation on the question of religion. I tried to pray with them, but I could not feel much spirit in the effort, and the heavens seemed as brass over my head. I

was discouraged and disheartened, and finally came to
the conclusion that it was no use to build a fire, and open
the house, just for myself. So during the last few days of
the meetings, I went to the school-house at the appointed
time, and knelt down behind the building and prayed for
that people.

During the meetings, (if you could call them meetings,)
I used to go into the store quite frequently, as I stayed
most of the time with the merchant; and there they used
to swear "by rule," as they say. I know some of them
would swear purposely to annoy me. I used to feel like
crying, and then again I would think that it was because
I was such a poor Methodist preacher, that I was not
worthy of anything better. If I was a better and more
worthy preacher they would respect me. After coming to
such a conclusion, I would take it as my just dues and try
to feel contented with it. But some would say, "why did
you go in there? What made you stay there?" It seemed
as though the more they ill-treated me the more I wanted
to be there. The merchant dare not say anything to
them, and it would not have done any good for me to
open my mouth there. One day when the merchant and
I were alone, I asked him if I could tack up one of the
commandments on the side of the store back of the stove.
He gave me the permission to do so and furnished a sheet
of light-colored paper, and I printed on it, as best I could,
with ink and pencil, the commandment against swearing,
and tacked it upon the wall. After that, especially if I
was in there, if anyone would swear, someone would
point to the notice on the wall, and then they would do

THE GRAVES SCHOOL-HOUSE.

more swearing than ever in their surprise. It sometimes made me almost ashamed that I had tacked it up, for they seemed to turn and rend me. All this time I was trying to hold meeting in Graves with my hands and feet tied. After two weeks of *my own revival* I stopped what I had even started, if there was anything to stop. I had prayed for them and had tried to talk with them and, having done all I could, I was confident that my object was pure, and that I was not to be blamed so much for my seeming failure.

And, yet, I did take all of the blame myself. Having failed I thought that the whole fault was with me, and that God had forsaken me, and that I was not worthy to be a minister. It seemed to me that if God cared for me, and I was his servant, that he would not let me be defeated so utterly. I hung my "harp upon the willows" and sat down and wept. I thought that when God would not help me there was no use in my trying to be a preacher, so I was ready to give up the work. I went to Graves with my head up, and my heart full of confidence in a certain and easy victory over old Jericho, and I came back from there with my head under my arm and my heart down in my boots, and no sign of a victory. I had got to take thirteen trips around the city, and the seven days of marching with the ridicule of Jericho and then shout and *see* the walls fall down, instead of being made strong enough to *pull down* the walls with *my own* hands. All of these things I had to learn.

I always called that meeting *my own revival*, for it seemed that I was going alone; and, then too, I accomplished not a thing of myself. My prayers, however, God heard, and in time were answered to the glory of God and the joy of my own heart.

THE SUNDAY SCHOOL ORGANIZED AT THE GRAVES' APPOINTMENT.

CHAPTER VII.

Graves had no Sunday-school nor anything else very religious, not even a collection. So one day in the spring, when the roads had settled a little, some of the young people came to church, so I thought I would organize a Sunday-school. We put a young man in for superintendent, who of course was "not a Christian," as some one said to me afterwards, in surprise at what I had done. Well! The next time that I came to preach, which was two weeks after, I learned that the Sunday-school died the preceeding Sabbath without even a dose of patent medicine to help it, nor even a prayer at the death and funeral of the same. So things were just the same as they had been before. The school did not live long enough to interest anybody, and consequently was not missed when it died, poor thing. A few weeks after another one was organized, and it was sickly when born, and soon died of heart disease. It only lived about ten days or so, and died for want of breath, poor thing. So when I came around afterwards to preach I heard strains of music down in the grove, where the cornet band had met to discourse music to please the dancers, as well as other people, and the remains of the poor Sunday-school was down there too. Of course there was no preaching that day, but, with a heavy heart I went on my way to the next appointment with the music of the band and the shouts and laughter of the people echoing in my ears for half a mile or more on my way.

Later in the season a man came to me and said, "Elder, why don't you start a Sunday-school here?" Well, I said, I have started the school twice, and it went down and out each time; but, if you will agree to help me, I will try again. You go and tell the children and the people that we will organize a Sunday-school next time I preach here. He agreed to do it, and I went my way. At my next appointment there were twelve, all told, present, including one old maid, one old woman and the man who wanted the Sunday-school. So I organized a Sunday-school and we put the man in for superintendent. He did not know anything about conducting a school, so I wrote out a programme and it was tacked up in the school-house where all could read it. That was the beginning of better days in Graves. Of course we only had prayer once in two weeks in the Sunday-school, and that was when I was there, so it could live by drawing a breath once in two weeks, if not oftener. It soon became known at the other appointments that I had started a Sunday-school in Graves, and put in a wicked sinner and a man that went to dances as superintendent. Of course my cold friend, the local preacher, and some others had a great deal to say about it. Some even came to me and talked about it. My only reply to them was, that if they could find any passage of scripture that forbid a poor sinner the privilege of studying the Bible or helping others to study it, I would stand condemned.

The very ones that stood ready to find fault with me about an ungodly superintendent would not go and take charge of the work there. They had no earthly business in the church or out of it, but to stand around and growl at other folks for doing the best they could. Some one ought to invent a safety-valve for such mouths. They only had prayer of course, once in two weeks, and that was when I was there for my regular appointment. On the printed programme I had tacked up for the use of the superintendent was first, singing; second prayer. The children used to read it and then call the attention of the superintendent to the omission of prayer, which kept the man in a state of uneasiness most of the time, because he could not pray. They would run up after Sunday-school was closed and say: "You skipped one of those," and "You forgot to pray." That Sunday-school lived, thank the Lord. It was a healthy child. The work was growing fast and the numbers increased rapidly.

A matter happened about this time that gave a wonderful uplift to the school and the community, too. It was this: A picnic was proposed by myself for the whole charge. A union picnic. There were five schools on the charge. One called a union school. I proposed the matter in the school at Yale, as that was headquarters. The school agreed to it, except the local preacher, and a committee was appointed to invite the other schools and the time was fixed and the place chosen. I was selected as one of the committee. I then went to graves to spur up my new Sunday-school to go to a picnic. They were ready to accept and join in the festivities. We had decided in the arrangements to have the band from Graves attend the picnic, too. So the Graves' school concluded to accompany the band to the grove. They had no banners for the school, so I secured some muslin and a carpenter made two poles, and I painted two nice mottoes, one for the little children, and one for the whole school. Each school was to furnish a part of the programme. So the Graves people were taking the matter in hand to furnish some speaking and singing, etc. It was the first time that any of the children had taken part in anything connected with a Sabbath-school, so they went to work with a will for fear they would not appear as well as the other schools.

In the meantime, the local preacher had gone to one of the other schools we were to invite—the union school—and persuaded one of his friends to propose that they get up a union picnic and invite the other schools to it, and they carried the measure and fixed the time on the day we had selected and the place, and sent invitations to the school at Yale and at Graves and took the whole matter out of the hands of the committee and of the Yale Sunday-school. The people at Graves were indignant over the

turn of affairs and said they would not go, and the band
said they would not go either. The Yale school did not
care much about it. I did not care, only it was a case of
well-settled meanness. So I said to the people of Graves
we must all go. Everybody turn out and make a show.
Let people know that there is something left yet in Graves
worth looking after. So they went to work harder than
ever. I was entirely set aside and left out altogether and
that troubled the people of Graves more than anything
else. But I told them that I did not care.

When the day came for the picnic we had a great
crowd of people in Graves; everybody turned out far and
near, and we had a long procession. The band took the
lead with the flag flying over their heads and two banners
in the procession. We started so as to be there on time,
but when we came to the grove they had commenced the
exercises without us, thinking we would not amount to
much. The band boys were angry, so they struck up a
lively tune and we went into the grove and marched into
the crowd, which of course stopped the programme, and
stopped one of the speakers in the middle of a piece. It
took some time to get things quiet again after such
a break. The local preacher looked quite uneasy. The
largest crowd of the day came from Graves. Their part
of the programme was as good and as well rendered as
any of those that tried to look down on the people from
Graves.

The people felt bad. It was not treating them as
Christian people ought to have treated sinners even, of
the worst sort; they tried to be cheerful and enjoy them-

selves, but they could not forget the way they had used me. They went home thinking that the preacher thought more of them than the rest of the church did, (although not many of the members, if any, save one family approved of the course taken by the Union Sunday-school,) and that the Sunday-school in Graves should be the best school on the charge. The next Sabbath the House was full for Sunday-school. Parents went to school, children went, and even Catholics came to the school. They were going to stand by the preacher now, he had stood by them for half a year, and now they are going to have a different state of things in graves. In a short time the school was by a considerable the largest school on the charge.

The superintendent was a sinner too, and running the most interesting school anywhere in that region.

Sometime late in the summer I held a grove meeting, and the superintendent was there. He generally went to church after he took charge of the Sunday-school. (We will call him Johnson, although that was not his real name, for I would not disclose the name.)

I could not let Johnson alone after the Sunday-school was organized. I was ever preaching to him, without intending to do anything of the kind. I could never be with him five minutes that I was not talking to him about his sinful life. Sometimes he would go with me to my evening appointment, and he would declare that I was preaching at him all the while during the meeting, which, of a truth, I had not thought of doing. I could not let him alone, for it seemed to me that he must be converted.

So, when he came to the grove meeting, he was hit so

hard that he thought it about time to get out of the way of the sword of the spirit, so, when I was through preaching on the Saturday afternoon of the meeting, he got up and burst into tears and begged of us to pray for him. We had a glorious meeting, and I was happy, and so was Johnson, too. Now, I said to him, we will have prayer in Sunday-school every Sunday; but he felt so weak that he tried to beg off, but I said to him, you just open school with prayer tomorrow and have it over with right off. He went home that night to get ready for Sunday-school. The next day was the Sabbath. We had a good meeting but my thoughts were constantly turning to the Sabbath-school and to Johnson.

During the afternoon prayer-meeting Johnson came and was so eager to let me know that he had prayer in Sunday-school that day, that he came right through the crowd and straight up to me and whispered it in my ear, and then we praised the Lord.

HOW I GAVE UP THE WORK.

CHAPTER VIII.

I had a habit of blaming myself for every little failure on the charge. And when I felt condemned for anything, then I was sure to declare myself unfit for the ministry. The local preacher did not seem to help me any, but rather hinder me in my work. He would not attend his own church but would get up a big ox load of people and go some where else to church, either to the Protestant church or the Seventh Day Baptist church or even the Free-Methodist church. I began to think that perhaps it was all my fault and that I must be wrong. So I thought my work must be done. I had some great struggles to settle the question beyond any new doubt that might arise from some new circumstances that I was truly called to the ministry. Some times I would pray for God to let me know, if I was called to that work, by letting me have a good time on the next Sabbath day when I went to preach. And God always gave me a great blessing at such times. So after a while I was not tempted by the Devil upon my call to the ministry. Then my temptations took a new form.˙ I was called to the work, but had I not finished my work and was not the state of the work such that I might well think my work done, and hence, I could go at some other business? And, yet, while I was made to see things in such a state, in fact, the work was in a blaze at most of the appointments. The Graves' Sunday-school was in a flourishing condition and congregations were good at every place. But the Devil made me think that because that local preacher would not come to church and stand by me that my work was all done up in shape, and I could go. One Sunday just before I had concluded that my work was done the local preacher and another man contradicted me after my sermon on a trivial point in regard to Zacheus climbing a sycamore tree to see the Lord pass by. They did not care so much about the point in question as they did the truth that I hooked on to that point. If they could break that point down the truth that came after it they thought would be weakened. What I had said was the eternal truth and I had not intended any personality, and did not know that I had hit them until they began to walk lame and flop one wing. Everybody else knew how bad they were too and applied the truth to them and stood up for me. Well, I made up my mind that the Lord had got through with me and my work was done, and so one morning I told the lady I boarded with that I was going to stop preaching. She cried and begged of me not to give up. But I had made up my mind, and I was going to know nothing but that determination henceforth. So I left my things there until I could find some employment. I went to the city and obtained a job with a friend of mine, securing articles for plating. I felt miserable and condemned. Something kept me thinking I was a Methodist preacher, and I was trying to forget it. People I knew would call me elder and that bothered me, for I was not going to be a preacher any longer. I finally bought a cigar and began to smoke, as I started out in the country, so as to divest myself of any appearance of a minister. I tried to feel mean and think mean but it was hard work.

When I would see some one coming, I would, before I thought, take my cigar out of my mouth lest they would see a preacher smoking, and then I would say I am not a preacher, and put it back in my mouth.

I went to a house and knocked at the door, and I tried to think I was an agent on the road, but something would tell me I stood on those steps a Methodist preacher. When I got into the house it was hard work to keep from saying something religious. I tried to obtain spoons and knives and forks for plating, but with such a struggle I was not fit to solicit anything from anyone. I tramped all day and obtained nothing for my toil. I was sick, miserable and defeated. I thought it strange that, if my work was done in the gospel, the Lord would defeat me in everything else. I finally came back to my boarding place after three days, and yet I had not came to the conclusion that I had better go to preaching again. I sat in my room fighting against conviction for some time, and

I kept saying I will not preach any more. While I was thus resolving in my mind some wondrous power took hold of me, and I began to weep. It came like a thunderbolt, and yet after weeping, I said I will not preach again.

At evening the class-leader and his wife and his son and wife came down. They had heard that I was discouraged and was going to give up the ministry. The more they talked to me the more I resolved to preach to them no more. Finally they wanted me to go home with them, and I said no. For I was not a Methodist preacher now, and it would be no use to go. They got my hat and put it on my head and lifted me into the wagon and took me home with them in spite of my refusals. After they had talked a while they concluded that I had better go to bed and rest over it. So the class-leader sang a hymn and called on me to pray, but I refused to pray; so they knelt down and prayed for me, and I began to realize how awful my sin, if I should drive the spirit from my heart, who had come to me so tenderly and lovingly and staid with me when I was trying to run away from my duty. And then the thought that I had refused to pray made me feel bad, and I said on my knees: Lord, I will obey! I then offered prayer before I arose. The struggle was over, and I got hold of God by a strong grip and held on while God put his arms of love about me and blessed me. I, like Jonah, had three miserable days. I was not in the whale's belly, but if Jonah felt any worse than I did, he certainly had a hard time of it. And I do not wonder that he started from the belly of the whale straight for Nineveh. He got all he wanted. I had all I wanted of disobedience.

I left Tuesday, and when Sunday came I was in my place to preach the gospel as usual, and the Lord blessed me, too. How far I went from God in my rebellion! and yet I was back again before Sunday. The Lord had mercy on me. The rest of my year was full of sunshine, and blessings came like rain drops.

GOING TO A "GREENBACK" MEETING.

CHAPTER IX.

While I was engaged in work for the Sabbath-school at Graves and doing pastoral visiting, I was invited to attend a Greenback meeting which was to be held in a neighboring town of considerable size. The gentleman who invited me said that I could ride down and back with him, so I accepted the invitation. Many loads went from Graves to the meeting, together with the band. The band was a new band about a year old, and could play well.

The meeting was the first one that the Greenbackers had in that vicinity and many bands and many people were present. After the meeting was over the band from Graves was led about town to play for the benefit of the whisky men and saloon-keepers. I went to the hotel where the gentleman who brought me put up his team and waited for him. He came late and had friends with

him who came that night on the train and who expected
to go out with him. He informed me that he would be
unable to take me and thought that I could get a ride
with some one else. But there seemed to be no chance left
for me but the big band-wagon. The driver said that I
could ride as well as not. So I waited for the band-wagon.
The band boys seemed about ready to go too. Then some
one proposed that the band should go over the town and
play for the hotels and saloons before going home. Some
of them were drinking quite freely, too, and all of them
were smoking. Away they went to play on the streets
and in the hotels and saloons. At every place they stopped
the proprietor treated them to whiskey, beer and cigars.
It took until after midnight to go around. All of this
time I was waiting at the hotel for the wagon to start.
When the boys came back to the starting place some were
very noisy and others very stupid, and the sober ones had
to work for an hour or more to get the boys to load up
for home. I was so ashamed of my company, and, if I
had been in the possession of money enough to pay my
expenses I would have staid there all night than be in such
a noisy, swearing crowd. I would have walked home, but
it was seven miles, or more, and the roads were quite
muddy, and it was a very dark night. So when the
wagon was ready to start a young Methodist preacher
was one of the crew. I pulled my hat down over my face
as far as possible and humped my back and took a seat
in the back end of the wagon and behind the one next in
front of me, so as to not be where the light from the torch
in the front of the wagon would show my face to anyone.

I hated myself and all about me. And I thought, as I was riding there, now everybody will hear of this, and that will be the end of my work as a Methodist preacher. Such language would hardly become a devil, as I heard that night. They swore and talked filthy and sang songs and cracked jokes, and anything else that suited their fancy was also added. We had to go through the place I called headquarters in order to reach Graves, where I was laboring then. When we went through Yale they made all the noise that it was possible to make. Those full of whiskey and beer yelled like loons.

I thought to myself what will the people say and the members of the church when they hear that the pastor of the M. E. Church was one of the number that went through town making such a noise in the small hours of the night. I prayed God to forgive me for my foolishness. Why did not I borrow some money and stay at the hotel all night; or why did not I sleep under the fence some where? I did think some of getting off, and then, if I did, I was sure that they would tell about me being one of their number, and, as I was spoiled for a Methodist now, I might as well ride with them as go "afoot."

Some of those in the front of the wagon did not know for a long time that the elder was in the load, but some sudden jerk of the wagon threw me into the light, and when they saw me one of them exclaimed with a terrible oath that the elder was in the wagon. Others replied with great oaths in astonishment at the new discovery made, and looked to see whether it was so or not.

I hung my head and hid behind my nearest neighbor,

who, by the way, was a sober man and a true friend to me. I was ready to give up all, for I thought there was no use of my trying to even be a Christian any longer.

The swearing and songs and talk went on just as before, and I thought it made no difference now for I was not a Methodist preacher any longer, so let them swear. It seemed as though all the angels in heaven were ashamed of me, and that Christ, my Savior, was blushing in shame for me, who had brought a reproach upon the ministry and the whole church.

I thought of the converts and what they would say about my kind of company. When we finally reached our destination, I jumped out and was crawling off in the darkness to get out of sight as soon as possible, when the merchant, who rode next to me and behind whom I kept hid most of the journey, overtook me, and wanted to know where I was going. I told him I did not know. He took me by the arm and said "you go and stay with me tonight." So I went to his house and went to bed, but not much sleep for me that night, that is, what was left of it.

The next band-meeting was a few nights after my sorry time; and when they met, they discussed the affair and came to the conclusion that it was time to have a change of the programme. So they made some new laws that night. One of the rules was that they would not play for a hotel or a saloon again; and another one was that whenever they played away from home again they were to come right home as soon as their engagement should be filled; and the other one was that the members of the band should use no profane or obscene language or get drunk under a fine of five dollars for every offense.

Then they came to me and told me what they had done.

I found out afterwards that I was safe enough as to my reputation, for they were all too much ashamed of themselves to ever mention the matter to anyone, and I certainly had no intention of telling anyone; and as far as I know no person outside of the band and myself ever knew of my experiences that night, even while I was on the charge.

But my ride reformed the band, and they kept the rules they had made as long as I had any knowledge of the band. The good Lord made it a blessing where I was only looking for evil to come. I had also the good will and friendship of the whole band and they came to church, and took an interest in helping to raise my salary. Even all things worked for good.

"BRINDLE HILL" PRAYER MEETING.

CHAPTER X.

During my pastorate on this first charge, we were
well-supplied with opportunities to attend prayer-meetings. We had meetings some where nearly every night of
the week. They were not all located meetings but some
were shifted about within a radius of ten miles or less and
others were fixed as permanent meetings. One of these
regular appointments was at the church, and the other
one was on the summit of "Brindle Hill," as one of the
brethren named it.

This hill had been burned over and it looked rather
streaked, as the fire did not burn the grass all off but left
it in streaks. Where the fire burned the grass the hill
looked brown; so one of the brethren named it "Brindle
Hill." On the top of this hill lived an old couple. In some
way we got a meeting appointed at their house and it
stayed there every week. They were poor and old. The

house consisted of one room about sixteen by eighteen feet. It was not lathed and plastered either on the sides or over head. They had both set by the stove day after day and night after night for many years and smoked their pipes, until the smoke of their pipes and of the old broken stove had blackened the timbers and boards overhead as black as coal tar. There were two or three old chairs and two or three stools, and an old square table and two bedsteads in the room. When we used to hold a meeting there, they brought in boards and old benches and made seats of them. In this little, old blackened room we had some powerful meetings. During these meetings the old folks were soundly converted to God. The old man used to pray: "O, Lord; give us more uv yeer love." For he had been tasting in his old age the love of God.

I used to like the meetings very much. But I did not like the company. For we had more bedbugs than human beings at the meeting. In spite of bedbugs we had some meetings when the people would shout to the top of their voices sometimes. We used to stay there sometimes until about midnight. Always after attending those meetings I had to pick my clothes over, and I have often found underneath my necktie a colony of bedbugs. One night I was caught in a terrific storm while attending the prayer-meeting. I could not possibly get home that night, as the road was a bad road, even in daylight. So I was pressed to stay that night in that house, and preferred bedbugs and a shelter to exposure that night. I stayed. There were two beds in the room. So when I got ready to go to bed the old lady went out of doors and the old man set

down facing the fire with his pipe while I went to bed.
Then the old lady came in and they blew out the tallow
candle and they went to to bed. In the morning I stayed
in bed, like children do, until breakfast was ready. Then
the old lady took the outside of the house while I dressed.
After a scanty meal I started on my way home not much
the worse for my night's adventure with strange bed-
fellows.

People somehow got the idea that the meetings must
be held at that place all of the while, and some even
thought the meetings were better there than elsewhere. I
think they were about as good as any we had anywhere
on the charge. I used to sometimes say that we were
nearer heaven when up on the old hill. It was a delight
to us to meet in that old shanty for prayer. I have been
to meetings there when everyone would laugh and sometimes shout. I have even known them to lose consciousness for a short time. One night a couple of the brethren
were so happy that on the way home from the meeting
in company with me they began to hug each other, and
finally lay down on the ground and rolled under an old
rail fence in their efforts to embrace each other a little
more closely. We used to have all sorts of people at the
"Brindle Hill" meeting. The Free Methodist, the Advents,
Methodist Protestant and Methodist Episcopal, and
some that were not anything. A Free Methodist man
who had left the Methodist church to join that Free insti-
tution used to come to the meetings and try to run a Free
Methodist meeting. He used to get down and pray with
his hands spread out and arms at full length, and would

keep them going like a bird flopping its wings. It always took him a long time to wing out his prayer. One night he was so extremely long and tedious that we were all tired of his prayer, and no doubt but the Lord was weary of such illimitable prayers, so we sung him down and out. He was such a sweet-spirited man, to take his word for it, and such a perfect man and so perfected in love; but I noticed that after I started a hymn in the midst of his extended talk, he was capable of being ruffled in spirit as well as the rest of God's weak creatures.

One would have thought to hear him talk that he was so perfect that nothing could offend him. But it was easier to offend him than anyone else. He could change his spiritual thermometer from hot to cold with the greatest of ease, as though he were used to that trade. No doubt he was. When a man thinks he has found a state of grace, if it has the tendency to knock all of the good sense out of him, he had better investigate his so-called state of grace.

If Christianity does anything for man, it not only changes his operations in life, but it also gives him a better and clearer conception of things, and especially of things relating to the Christian life. It proves itself, when present in the heart, by that consideration it gives one, of the feelings and rights of others, and that Christian charity that "thinketh no evil" of others, who claim an interest and a hope in the merits of the Redeemer of mankind.

So when this man thought only of himself, and, like a pig getting lengthwise in the trough, preventing anyone else getting a mouthful, he wanted to use all of the time and snatch all of the cake from the table, I began to think that some of the lambs needed something as well as the pig, and so I started a lively hymn and all of the singers joined in, and his wings dropped to his side and his lower jaw dropped, and the noise of the "sounding brass and tinkling cymbal" ceased. He did not attend meetings with us for a long time after that, if he ever did. Some folks want all or they want nothing.

I have had occasion once or twice since then to sing down a windy saint. On one charge, I was holding a series of meetings and the people were getting very much aroused and awakened. There had been in the vicinity of the church some years before a Free Methodist class. Some old remnants of that class still remained. The most of those left came to my meetings and were getting into the work in good earnest. One old man with a little show of learning, and a poor show at that, had been termed "leader" by the Free Methodist. He looked after the Free Methodist flock, what there was of it. He did not come to the meetings for a long time. Finally a prayer-meeting one afternoon came within easy reach of this old "leader" and so he came. Not having attended the meetings any he was not in the drift of the work, but rather he was like an iceberg in a summer sea; the iceberg produced an effect upon the immediate sea, and in turn the sea effected the iceberg, and as it is slow work melting an icebers, so we found it in this case, too.

When he prayed he consumed about half an hour. He was not asking the Lord for anything, but he was instructing the Lord and reciting history to him. He told all he knew about Bible history. Among other things he told the Lord how one leaf of the Bible had been sold for a load of hay, as though the Lord did not know about it. He used up all of the time that we generally allowed for prayers. So I changed the order of the meeting. Then he got up and began to reel off another thousand mile thread, and when he had used up about half of the time I began to sing with all my might, and the thread broke and that stopped the reel.

You get about half a dozen such "long-winded" fellows together and you would need to begin the meeting after breakfast and have a lunch in your pocket for dinner and expect a late supper, if you staid all through the meetidg, and, too, a man would want a prod stuck into him every five minutes to keep awake, for they would put a maniac to sleep in ten minutes. Such men afford us good opportunities to cultivate the grace of patience and charity, but patience ceases to be a virtue before the sun goes down, if you begin in the morning with such fellows. Such are some of the things that come along in the current of human events to knock off the rough corners of mortal men in the ministry, and by friction put on a little of the shine. So that "all things work together for good," even if a man does not relish the thing, for the bitter medicine may give strength; but then I would rather take the medicine from choice than have it forced down my throat.

HOW I MADE THE CIRCUIT.

CHAPTER XI.

I made my circuit on foot. When I went onto the circuit I had a pair of leaky boots, and while they answered well enough for the sidewalks in a village, they were of no very great use on the roads and in the mud and water, if you desired to keep your feet dry and clean. It was one of the worst winters for mud and water I have known since I have been in the work, too, and when I started off for an exploration on my charge I used to get my pants up on my boot tops and take my coat on my arm and my little, old Bible in my hand and a hymn-book and pick my way along the fences and over logs and across the fields and through the woods to reach my point.

The Bible, by the way, was the first Bible I ever had. It was given to me by a Sunday-school teacher as a Christmas present on a tree, when I was a little boy. It cost about forty cents, as that is the price of the book as marked on the cover; for the mark is there yet.

In my journeys sometimes it was necessary to cross the road in order to proceed, and it was not always a very pleasant duty. I remember having on a pair of rubbers once, that were none too tight, and being obliged to cross the road I started to cross in a place that looked to be sandy. I got into the middle of the road and the first I knew I began to sink in the quick sand. I lifted up one foot and the rubber came off. I took my books under my arm and tried to put my rubber on, but when I had it on, the other foot had gone out of sight. I then tried to get that foot out and the rubber came off and so I had to work again standing on one foot. I lost my balance and had to put my foot down without the rubber on in order to save myself. The other rubber came off and I was getting deeper in the mire, so securing my rubbers in my hands I pulled for the fence as best I could. I came very near getting in over my boot tops. What a plight I was in; the mud plastered all over my boots and some on my best pants, and those were not very good either.

By the time I had gone seven or eight miles in such weather and with such roads as I had then, I was in a sorry plight. About the first thing was asking the privilege of taking off boots and stockings and cleaning up when I stopped for good, if indeed I did not have to borrow a suit of clothes for a day. Many a time I have crawled into some one else's boots and pants while I dried and cleaned my own.

Sometimes I have been out in the night with no place

to go for the night but my boarding place, perhaps five miles away. I have been to prayer-meeting and staid until late in the evening, and no one invite me home for the night, as they each thought I was going with the other, I suppose, and so I have walked five miles in the dark, sometimes so dark I had to feel my way along the road. Of course during such journeys I was not able to pick out my way, but plough through. My big feet have many times come down in the middle of some deep mud hole in the middle of the road making the water fly all over me. I used to be very thankful that no one could see me when I steamed into port in the evening.

Sometimes I have been out in the night when a heavy shower would come up and I would get soaked clean to the hide, if even the hide did not get soaked. That was a year in which I could not dress very well for two reasons. First, I had not the money to buy anything, better with, and secondly, if I had, it would have been folly to put anything on worth much to be caught out in, as I was so many times that year.

My salary was very limited that year, so that I was not able to buy a horse, not even a saw horse. I used to fill my appointmsnts regularly, however, and generally on time. What little money I did get had to go for boots and rubbers and for books and papers and for letter paper etc. I believe I was poorer when the year was up than when I began my work, not only in pocketbook but in flesh. I walked-off all the flesh, and was thin, and gaunt, and my clothes were as rib-bare as I was. But I was happy and I believe I could say truthfully "blessed be nothing." I had nothing to worry over, only lest my pants should give out on the knees or elsewhere to my discomfort.

I was poor when I went on to the circuit, and poor when I went away from it. I had very little money that first year. The people were poor and the families were large and the preacher had to take what he could get. I find on one page of my book for that year, that one farmer is credited for himself and family with the following :

3 ℔s. butter...$	.84
½ bushel potatoes...	.20
6 ℔s. meat........................:.........................	.50
½ bushel apples...	.25
Total...$1.79	

Another one (a sister) 1 pair of socks....................$	.40
The local preacher, 1 cord of wood (slabs)...............	1.00
One old lady 7 ℔s. meat...................................	.85

That is about the way it run through the year. I was single and boarding, and could turn most of the truck over to my landlady. My salary for the year did not exceed $250 including everything. I was not able therefore to secure even a horse to ride. So I was the circuit rider on foot. I used to preach at Yale in the morning, and then walk five miles to the Jones school-house for the afternoon and to Graves seven miles for evening. Then the next Sabbath, I would preach at Maple school-house in the morning and then take up one of the other appointments in the afternoon and another one in the evening, giving me plenty of exercise during the day. I was not troubled any with the dyspepsia nor the gout. I wore out plenty of sole-leather though, and sweat out many paper collars.

During a part of the winter I was permitted to ride a colt. A very wicked man took pity on the "circuit walker" and said if I would come down to his house he would let me have a colt to ride. So I went down and rode the colt home to my boarding place. I borrowed a bridle of the old man who owned the colt and a saddle of a neighbor, and I felt as big as a King on a throne, when I left town on the back of a colt. I made good use of the colt while I kept it. For about three months anyway I was a real "circuit rider." I did more walking that first year of my ministry than I have the thirteen following years. I did not mind the walking any, for I was walking for the Lord, and I was well paid for all of my labor. I waded mud, walked on logs and fence rails and built pontoon bridges across turbulent, swelling torrents (or some other kind of a bridge) that I might carry the gospel into the "regions beyond me." I was a veritable gospel-peddler and carried the gospel into every house. I boarded around among the people; I had to. The people thought I must. The extent of my circuit compelled me to live with the people much, and my salary was so meager that I could not have staid there unless I did.

I was thoroughly acquainted with my people. I knew their home life. Quite a number of times I helped my people establish the family altar in their homes. Afoot, or on horseback, I meant to do my duty with the help of the Lord. I believe I did do my duty, too. God lifted up my head above mine enemies round about me, and I was full of joy, and was enabled to preach with power.

Many times I have preached with wet feet and soiled clothing and wrinkled collar, with my clothing wet with sweat from my journey. I always forgot my ills (if such they could be called) when I began to preach, and the Lord used to bless my words. Sometimes everyone in the house would be in tears—saint and sinner. Even now I look back upon that year as a green spot in my ministerial life that will never fade away.

If tramping would give me the same power and the same pay and the same sweet experience, together with its clouds and sunshine, I would be willing to pull off my shoes and pull on my kipp boots and take the road. Every year has been a good year, however. But I was a babe in the ministry then, and to a man no time is so sweet as his childhood days, with its clouds and sunshine and songs and tears.

I have been singing doxologies ever since that first year at the remembrance of God's goodness to me, and the blessings and victories of my initiation into this the noblest work in which man can engage.

SUMMARY.

CHAPTER XII.

At the end of the year my charge was in a warm and
flourishing condition. At Yale the work had become
quite satisfactory. I had taken on probation during the
year 39 persons. Many of them had come into the church
in full connection before the year was up; and the most of
the remainder were still on the way. The Seventh Day
Baptists were not doing as well at the end of the year as
they expected. Things did not turn out as they expected
they would when they set up business against the Methodist Episcopal church. They did not start right. If they
had any noisy work to do they always seemed to do it on
the Sabbath day, and get as near the church to do it, or
some conspicuous place, where it would annoy the first-
day people. For instance, one fine Sabbath day when the
people were coming to church the leading man in the
Baptist church got out in the road to clean his stovepipe

so that people could see and hear the noise as they were going to church.

Like the old woman and the preacher whom she thought needed snuffing. The preacher arose in a sleepy way and read in a drawling manner his text, which was this: "I am the light of the world." Then he repeated the text, after looking about upon the audience. When he had finished the text for the second time, "I am the light of the world," an old lady piped out in a squeaky voice, "If you *are*, you need *snuffing*." So if that man with his stovepipe was one of God's lights he needed snuffing badly.

The Free Methodists did a good deal of shouting and exercising, but that only kept them from being dyspeptic, while it did not result in any marked degree in the growth of that church or the overthrow of the Methodist Episcopal church, which ever has been, and probably always will be, an eye-sore to the bulk of that society. They verily thought we were all hypocrits. Perhaps we were, but we were having a glorious time of it, and if that kind of feeling comes from hypocracy, like the dutchman, who, addmitted that money was the root of all evil, (which of course it is not) said, "but give me some more of the root," so I say give us some more of that kind of hypocracy.

The Advents, both the First Day and the Seventh Day, were going about saying, that they were looking for Christ to come any day. One old man with long hair and a longer beard used to go around the neighborhood stroking his beard and declaring in funeral tones that he thought Christ would come any day now, for the end was near. Some of them even went so far as to pick out the farm they were going to live on after Christ had killed all of the wicked and purified the earth by fire. One farm they had an eye on was the property of a good old saint, but it was no matter to them, they were going to people the earth. I had a talk with one Advent, and he claimed that the spirit went into the grave with the body and staid there until the resurrection morn. I quoted scripture to him and he would claim that it was all wrong, and, when I see that he was not capable of furnishing any scripture in proof of his position and yet denied all that I offered, I asked him if he really believed that the spirit went into the grave? He said he did. Then I said, I hope the Lord will let you lay in the grave with the dust and old dry bones, if you really believe it, I am not going there anyway. The old fellow got mad at me, and would not speak to me nor go to my meetings after that. He did not seem to like his own medicine very well. The whole time of those *would-be saints* is taken up with some point that will not make one hair whiter nor blacker. To me, to help someone get ready to meet the Lord when he comes is far above trying to convince someone that he is coming tomorrow or next day. It is none of our business when he comes, if it was, the Lord would have told us all about it, but our business is to be always ready, for we know not when he will come. Somethings are important. The preaching of faith, repentance, regeneration, the work of the spirit, the love of God and our duties to God and one another are worth more to the ounce than all the disputed and distinguishing points of all the churches put together are worth by the shipload dumped on the docks. How much corn will a man husk in a day if he stops to discuss the formation of a husk? The husks are necessary, but only because of the corn on the ear. Some people are always stripping husks and getting no corn. Let us have the corn!

Away with those old bones—old fossils of dead faith and rotten reason. What this hungry, crying world wants is bones with meat on them. You never saw a man that was gnawing an old weather-worn bone that was very fat. When you meet one of these old bone-eaters, you only find a shadow of a man. He may try to persuade you to eat, and tell you how delicious it is, but if you do accept his bone you will be nothing more spiritually than skin and bones.

Some animals can seem to thrive in a grave-yard. Go into the grave-yard of the past and you can find the fossils of old dead isms, that have been left there after the birds have picked off what little meat there was on them.

Christianity comes to the soul full of juice, fresh and palatable. The soul that feeds upon the gospel will be fat. Health, freshness, beauty and strength become those who are well-fed. God's people are well-fed. "They shall be fat and flourishing."

I thank God that I never tried to feed my people on dry bones bleached in the sun of centuries. We went in for the marrow of the gospel. If we were cut short sometimes in this world's goods we never were in want for the delicacies of that other world.

In my experiences boarding around, I often came to

hard fare. Sometimes I have dined on salt and potatoes, sometimes on poor bread with no butter; once I dined on stewed woodchuck, often on chickens and sometimes I did not get a chance to dine on anything. It was about the same with beds. Sometimes I would find good beds, other times I have slept on a straw tick that was so thin that the slats that held up the tick amounted to a great deal more by way of close fitting, than the straw in the tick. Sometimes I have examined the beds in the morning to see if they had put any stuffing in the ticks or not. I have gotten up in cold weather and put my clothes on and gone back to bed to keep warm, and, like Paul and his company when on the stormy sea, wished for the daybreak.

But those things did not hinder my work in the least, I could preach as well on stewed woodchuck as on cake and pie, and feel as strong for the battle after being stretched upon slats or bedcords for the rest and sleep of the night, as if on goose feathers.

With all of the unpleasant things connected with the work, I must say that my first year was a happy, triumphant year in my ministry and one never to be forgotten. I would not hesitate for one moment to go over the same road again with the same blessed scenes, associations and experiences, with few exceptions, and one of those the bedbugs. What I mean is that the exceptions are not taken in regard to any of the blessed things, but in respect simply to some of the associations, mentioned above.

In conclusion, let me say, that the life of a preacher is

not a life all sunshine nor all shadows, but it is such a Divine combination of the two that one at once loses sight of the one in the brightness of the other. And, believing that all things will work together for good to them that love God, the preacher clings to the ship and lets God take the helm, and thus out-rides the storm. In that sense all should be preachers and cling to the ropes. We may not be able to save a cause, but this mighty, glorious cause will save all who cling to it.

THE END.

A few Original Poems.

THE OLD FLINT-LOCK MUSKET.

(Parody on " The Old Oaken Bucket.")

How painful the memories linked with my childhood,
　While fond recollections there seems but a few;
The tree with green apples, that tasted so bitter
　And gave me the cramps and the stomachache, too;
The wide-spreading pond where I spoiled my new breeches,
　And stuck myself fast in the deep, quaking mire;
The hand of my father that used to fit tightly,
　And warmed my thin trousers as if in the fire,
And then that old musket, the rusty old musket,
　My grandfather's musket that stood in the barn.

That old rusty musket I hail with no pleasure;
　For one time at noon, when returned from the store,
I found it the source of a thousand bad speeches
　And groanings and bruises a thousand times more;
How ardent I seized it, my grandfather's musket,
　And quick to my shoulder I brought the old stock,
And soon as I pulled at the rusty old trigger
　The thunder and lightning burst forth all at once;
My heels took the air and I cut a queer figure,
　While stars danced about me a million or more.

How bitter my thoughts, and how wild the commotion,
　When I think of the musket that stands in the barn;
Not a mine of rich treasures could tempt me to touch it,
　Though foes should assail me or threaten me harm;
My revenge would be sweeter if my foes took the musket,
　For the danger is greater behind than before.
When ever I think of my father's plantation
　That rusty old musket comes up in my mind,
The war with old England they called "Revolution;"
　And since I revolved so I know what it means.

HIS MERCY ENDURETH FOREVER.

I will sing to the Lord a new song,
  Giving thanks for his goodness to me;
Unto Him, who is mighty and strong,
  Unto Him all the glory shall be.
    For His mercy endureth,
    Yes, endureth forever.

He unlocked the embrace of the wave,
  That his people in safety might pass;
While their enemies found but a grave,
  As the waves sought each other's embrace.
    For His mercy endureth,
    Yes, endureth forever.

In the desert His people He led,
  And made waters gush forth from the rock;
And with manna His people were fed:
  For He leadeth and feedeth His flock.
    For His mercy endureth,
    Yes, endureth forever.

ALL ALONE.

In the darkness all alone,
 While the night winds sadly moan;
With no cheering gleam of light,—
Wand'ring, wand'ring in the night.

Weary, weary, all alone,—
Threat'ning clouds are sweeping on;
But no shelter from the storm;
With no friend, alone to roam.

Sinner, list! There is a call,
From the distance,—O, so small,—
Lo! A star,—O, turn and see,—
Shining now for thee, for thee.

Jesus calls,—O, sinner come,
He's prepared for thee a home;
Flee from danger, flee from harm,
Come to Christ's dear, loving arms.

THE KICKER OF HONEYMOON CIRCUIT.

There was a hard place called Honeymoon Circuit,
And they wanted a *new man* to work it;
And so the wise Bishop sent on a *new preacher*,
To be their next pastor and teacher.

But the *new one* was too *old* to accept him,—
And the preacher *was single* that left them;
And thus the P. E. did arrange it,
So he could quite easily change it.

The change it was made; the preacher sent on,—
The one they had seemed to be bent on;
They claimed to be very contented,
And a parsonage quickly was rented.

The bounds of the charge were far-reaching,
And five were the place for preaching;
The work was quite vast in proportions,
And sometimes beset with strange notions.

And one of these points was named Orlo,
Where things must be always *thus* or *so*.
Their piety run in an unknown direction,
Or else they were lacking the very best section.

The people of Orlo were thinking of yielding,
For the want of a proper church building;
And the *work* and the *cause* had been lagging,
And the faith of the saints seemed flagging.

The Classleader, "spokesman," "chieftain" and so-forth,
Was David Cantdoit, whose "bossly" go forth.
Was the word of command and the end of all lawing,
And it had to go forth without "*hemming* and *hawing*."

This David Cantdoit had "fixed up" the members,
Until they thought he was the "greatest of timbers."
They worshiped the man, they worshiped his money,
'Til the worship of God wasn't worth quite a penny.

They told the new preacher: "Perhaps you don't know it,
But we never could live without brother Cantdoit."
One would think from the talk of this silly, blind people,
That "brother Cantdoit" was the god on the steeple.

The preacher, he worshiped the Lord God, Almighty,
The people, "David Cantdoit," the conceity;
And so it's no wonder the people were lagging,
And the faith of the saints was flagging.

But "brother Cantdoit" said the trouble with Orlo,
Was the want of a church either *thus* or *so*;
" We want a new church; it is now or never,"
The others said; "Yes, it is now, if ever.

The preacher never bowed down to "brother Cantdoit,"
And this worldly-wise saint seemed to know it;
And being more mulish than saintly by nature,
He always objected to every new measure.

The preacher, in love for the *cause* and the *people*,
Proposed a new church, with belfry and steeple;
When up jumps the "Leader" and says: "We can't do it,"
Like all other skeptics he adds: "And I know it."

This man, who for reasons just told, talked of yielding,
Was the first to oppose the much-needed building.
He "*hemmed*" and he "*hawed*" and without any reason,
He said: ''*You Can't do it*," and "*This aint the season*."

The work went "ahead" by "lifting" and "tugging;"
But this *awful good man* made it very hard lugging;
He laid down and rode on top of the burden,
And growled that so long was the time to the Jordan,

If the work should succeed, he wanted the credit,
And if it should fail, the preacher would get it;
But, in truth, if it failed he deserved all the blaming,
And with its success he wasn't worth naming.

This "unsaintly" saint kicked as a source of his giving,
For kicking was part of his every-day living;
He aimed at the preacher with hatefulness ever,
As though he was certain it was "*now or never*."

When the preacher had finished his work, they dismissed him,
And not even a blessing for his work they wished him.
While many the hands that helped to receive him,
He must "go it alone," when the time comes to leave them.

As of yore, there was a cry from Honeymoon Circuit;
For they wanted a *new man* to work it.
And God pity the man that meets with such foes,—
They are glad when he comes, and pleased when he goe s.

But David Cantdoit will find he *can't do it*,
And the angels in heaven all know it;
For kicking doth make him a dangerous rival,
And, if he keeps kicking, he'll go to the Devil.

TRUSTING IN THE LORD.

I have found a safe retreat;
I can all my foes defeat,
    Trusting in the Lord.
Joshua, the victory man,
David's mighty deeds were done,
    Trusting in the Lord.

Jesus spake the Holy word,
Wond'rous news the peple heard,
    Trusting in the Lord.
Blind men had their sight restored,
Health and strength the sick implored,
    Trusting in the Lord.

Cripples took their beds and walked
'Mid the throngs where Jesus talked,
    Trusting in the Lord.
Vile men had their sins forgiven,
And they started out for heaven,
    Trusting in the Lord.

Weeping Mary Jesus sought:—
From the tomb good news she brought,
    Trusting in the Lord.
Christ's apostles preached with power,
Had a "pentecostal shower."
    Trusting in the Lord.

JUST CALL AND SEE FOR YOURSELVES.

Written in 1876.

[This poem was suggested by an advertisement in a newspaper, offering great bargains, etc , and closed by saying "Just Call and see For Yourselves.]

The storehouse of God is full and free,—
    Just call and see for yourselves;
The door stands ajar for you and me,—
    Just call and see for yourselves.
The Bible describes its stock of gold,
Its value to you can never be told,—
    Just call and see for yourselves.

The bargains are great, and it will pay,—
    Just call and see for yourselves;
You never should doubt what thousands say,—
    Just call and see for yourselves.
No money is needed when you go,
The firm is so rich, they give, you know,—
    Just call and see for yourselves.

There is a full line of gospel fare,—
    Just call and see for yourselves;
And there is a stock of blessings rare,—
    Just call and see for yourselves.
There is but one price on everything,
And that has been paid by Christ, the King,—
    Just call and see for yourselves.

A SING'LAR CUSTOM.

(A parody on the " New Church Doctrine.")

There is a sing'lar custom, Sue,
    Among our folks to-day;
'Tis not in whole a thing so new,
    So all the preachers say;—
That literal, everlastin' howl,
    As if about to die,
Some people always have to growl
    At everything we try.
I doubt somewhat about that clime,
    They always talk about,
A bein' quite "so mild" sometime,
    As they may yet find out.

I've watched my duty, straight an' true,
    An' tried to do it well;
I always gave with Christ in view,
    An' always made it tell.
But some will sing—an' give just naught—
    "A foll'wer of the Lamb;"
An' all the battle they have fought,
    Is only just a whim.
Great are the dangers I have braved,
    The sacrifice it cost;—
An' now if these ere folks are saved,
    My sacrifice is lost.

Just think! To say they "mean to do,
    An' help the cause along,
'His track I see, an' I'll pursue,'"
    Is brother Tubbs's song.
An' talks about the narrow way,
    As if he walked beside the King;
Au' looks at me as if to say,
    "Don't you wish you could sing?"
But when the plate is passed around,
    He lays it on so still,—
As if a cent would give a sound
    His very soul to ctill

An' there is Deacon James and wife,
    They have no children left,
Au' they should carry in this life
    Of burdens quite a heft.
But when you ask them "to divide,"
    An' help the preacher on,
With thousands saved, right by their side,
    The preacher gets a "one."
They always say, "how much it costs
    To keep the meetin' up;"
But the church would be in ruin lost,
    Were they the only prop.

Old Captain Bates has never done.
    An' has his pockets crammed;
I sometimes think he'll be the one,
    If any one is damned.

An' Peter Flag did murmer so
　　An' said, "The times were hard,"
But he could go to Barnum's show,
　　An' buy a "family card."
There comes a thought I can't control,
　　That Satan may get some;—
He takes the purse to lead the soul
　　To his infernal home.

An' there was Smith lay sick and weak,
　　For many an' many a day,
And all because he sought to seek
　　An' lay more dimes away.
He had enough to last him through,
　　Nor do another thing;
An' now because—from follow too—
　　He had to "clip his wing."
The cause of Christ must suffer loss;
　　The preacher suffer lack,—
The man was sick, and so his cross
　　Will be to "brace his back."

But tears can never do my part,
　　Nor feed a hungry soul;
When love is in my inner heart,
　　My purse is in control.
I hold mine right side up with care,
　　To shield mine eyes from sin,
An' coax the Lord with daily pray'r,
　　To use the dimes within.
But if these grumblers won't draw nigh,
　　An' take salvation's plan,
I'll have to stand an, see 'em try
　　To dodge hell, if they can.

" BLESS ME !   THIS IS PLEASANT."

A poem composed at the age of 17 years.

[The subject called "Wat" was a hotel keeper of a very bad
sort, whose given name was Washington, and was always called
"Wat" and "Watty." He kept a very bad house and was strongly
opposed by temperance people. He was greedy for gain.]

As "Wat" sat by his bar-room fire,
And none but he was there,
He counted o'er the dimes he'd made
By his nefarious trade.
And as he laid them on the shelf,
Thus said he to himself:
How fast I'm making money,
In this land of beer and honey.
                Bless me! This is pleasant.

I know some people don't like me,—
With temperance folks I don't agree ;
They have their friends—*I have*, I think,
For there is Doctor Link
And Jessie Bench and Billy Dock,
Come each as steady as a clock.
O! how I'll scoop the money
And make the boys feel funny!
                Bless me! I am happy.

Now, there's my Farmers' Jubilee —
Some called it " Watty's spree,—
Just think! because we had some fun
They go howlin' round the town.
Well! humph! I made some money. Whew!
I guess I did—a bushel, too.
They all had lots of money,
And seemed to feel quite funny.
                Bless me! It was pleasant.

Because we had a pole to climb
Close by, to pass away the time,
Then some of those cold-water clams,
They scoffed at me like fighting rams,
And said I meant to sell out dry.—
The truth of that I don't deny—
For those who came had money,
And got to feeling funny;
                Bless me! It was pleasant.

Plague take those stiff cold-water men,
They call my place "The Devil's Den ;"
They fight against my honest trade.
As though I had no license paid.
I'll get their sons here on the sly,
As the spider did the silly fly,
And when I get their money
It won't seem quite so funny.
            Bless me! If I don't.

I went to a donation once—
A big consummate dunce,
To give the Rev., a Methodist,
A crisp new "V," just to assist;
And now he's fighting hard 'gainst me,
And voted temperance, too, I see;
He 'preciated my money
In a way that isn't funny.
            Bless me! It isn't pleasant.

Now there's that painter Buckman, too,
He's stiffer by far than my old shoe,
I wouldn't have had him paint for me,
But I thought of course the man could see,
That he could drink here on the sly
The best of whisky made of rye.
Good Templars ain't so funny,
For I don't get much of their money.
            Curse me! What a crowd!

Now some have said that I am, (hic,)
In town "sole agent for Old Nick."
Has Satan got on me a claim?
There is no justice, truth nor shame
In hurting thus my honest trade.
Away, then, to the midnight shade
With things that ain't so funny,
I am after the drinker's mon y.
            Curse me! If I don't get it.

And so old "Wat" went off to bed,
To wake at morn to ply his trade.
Old Elam came for his morning drink
And Dock and Bench and Doctor Link.

And so the days, the months went by,
And soon old " Wat" laid down to die,
If 'twas pleasant making money,
To die was not so funny,—
   Not quite so pleasant.

EVIL IMAGINATION.

A friend drops in so light,
  And says that neighbor B——
Intends to rob your house to-night,
  He often looks that way.
Now, on the strength of that
Be cat, and watch the rat,
Or he may gnaw a fearful hole,
And steal away your soul.